The Awful German Language

by

Mark Twain

Rise of Douai

ISBN-13: 978-1522732044

ISBN-10: 1522732047

Introduction

Samuel Langhorne Clemens (November 30, 1835 – April 21, 1910), better known by his pen name Mark Twain, was an American author and humorist. He wrote The Adventures of Tom Sawyer (1876) and its sequel, Adventures of Huckleberry Finn (1885), the latter often called "The Great American Novel".

Twain grew up in Hannibal, Missouri, which provided the setting for Huckleberry Finn and Tom Sawyer. After an apprenticeship with a printer, he worked as a typesetter and contributed articles to the newspaper of his older brother, Orion Clemens. He later became a riverboat pilot on the Mississippi River before heading west to join Orion in Nevada. He referred humorously to his singular lack of success at mining, turning to journalism for the Virginia City Territorial Enterprise. In 1865, his humorous story, "The Celebrated Jumping Frog of Calaveras County", was published, based on a story he heard at Angels Hotel in Angels Camp, California, where he had spent some time as a miner. The short story brought international attention, and was even translated into classic Greek. His wit and satire, in prose and in speech, earned praise from critics and peers, and he was a friend to presidents, artists, industrialists, and European royalty.

Though Twain earned a great deal of money from his writings and lectures, he invested in ventures that lost a great deal of money, notably the Paige Compositor, a mechanical typesetter, which failed because of its complexity and imprecision. In the wake of these financial setbacks, he filed for protection from his creditors via bankruptcy, and with the help of Henry Huttleston Rogers eventually overcame his financial troubles. Twain chose to pay all his pre-bankruptcy creditors in full, though he had no legal responsibility to do so.

Twain was born shortly after a visit by Halley's Comet, and he predicted that he would "go out with it", too. He died the day after the comet returned. He was lauded as the "greatest American humorist of his age", and William Faulkner called Twain "the father of American literature".

Twain began his career writing light, humorous verse, but evolved into a chronicler of the vanities, hypocrisies and murderous acts of mankind. At mid-career, with Huckleberry Finn, he combined rich humor, sturdy narrative and social criticism. Twain was a master at rendering colloquial speech and helped to create and popularize a distinctive American literature built on American themes and language. Many of Twain's works have been suppressed at times for various reasons. Adventures of Huckleberry Finn has been repeatedly restricted in American high schools, not least for its frequent use of the word "nigger", which was in common usage in the pre-Civil War period in which the novel was set.

A complete bibliography of his works is nearly impossible to compile because of the vast number of pieces written by Twain (often in obscure newspapers) and his use of several different pen names. Additionally, a large portion of his speeches and lectures have been lost or were not written down; thus, the collection of Twain's works is an ongoing process. Researchers rediscovered published

material by Twain as recently as 1995 and
2015.

The Awful German Language

THE AWFUL GERMAN LANGUAGE.

A little learning makes the whole world kin.—
Proverbs xxxii, 7.

I went often to look at the collection of curiosities
in Heidelberg Castle, and one day I surprised the
keeper of it with my German. I spoke entirely in that
language. He was greatly interested; and after I had
talked a while he said my German was very rare,
possibly a "unique;" and wanted to add it to his
museum.

If he had known what it had cost me to acquire my
art, he would also have known that it would break any
collector to buy it. Harris and I had been hard at work
on our German during several weeks at that time, and
although we had made good progress, it had been
accomplished under great difficulty and annoyance, for
three of our teachers had died in the meantime. A
person who has not studied German can form no idea
of what a perplexing language it is.

Surely there is not another language that is so slip-
shod and systemless, and so slippery and elusive to the
grasp. One is washed about in it, hither and hither, in
the most helpless way; and when at last he thinks he
has captured a rule which offers firm ground to take a
rest on amid the general rage and turmoil of the ten
parts of speech, he turns over the page and reads, "Let
the pupil make careful note of the following
exceptions." He runs his eye down and finds that there

are more exceptions to the rule than instances of it. So overboard he goes again, to hunt for another Ararat and find another quicksand. Such has been, and continues to be, my experience. Every time I think I have got one of these four confusing "cases" where I am master of it, a seemingly insignificant preposition intrudes itself into my sentence, clothed with an awful and unsuspected power, and crumbles the ground from under me. For instance, my book inquires after a certain bird—(it is always inquiring after things which are of no sort of consequence to anybody): "Where is the bird?" Now the answer to this question,—according to the book,—is that the bird is waiting in the blacksmith shop on account of the rain. Of course no bird would do that, but then you must stick to the book. Very well, I begin to cipher out the German for that answer. I begin at the wrong end, necessarily, for that is the German idea. I say to myself, "Regen, (rain,) is masculine—or maybe it is feminine—or possibly neuter—it is too much trouble to look, now. Therefore, it is either der (the) Regen, or die (the) Regen, or das (the) Regen, according to which gender it may turn out to be when I look. In the interest of science, I will cipher it out on the hypothesis that it is masculine. Very well—then the rain is der Regen, if it is simply in the quiescent state of being mentioned, without enlargement or discussion—Nominative case; but if this rain is lying around, in a kind of a general way on the ground, it is then definitely located, it is doing something—that is, resting, (which is one of the German grammar's ideas of doing something,) and this throws the rain into the Dative case, and makes it dem

Regen. However, this rain is not resting, but is doing something actively,—it is falling,—to interfere with the bird, likely,—and this indicates movement, which has the effect of sliding it into the Accusative case and changing dem Regen into den Regen." Having completed the grammatical horoscope of this matter, I answer up confidently and state in German that the bird is staying in the blacksmith shop "wegen (on account of) den Regen." Then the teacher lets me softly down with the remark that whenever the word "wegen" drops into a sentence, it always throws that subject into the Genitive case, regardless of consequences—and that therefore this bird staid in the blacksmith shop "wegen des Regens."

N. B. I was informed, later, by a higher authority, that there was an "exception" which permits one to say "wegen den Regen" in certain peculiar and complex circumstances, but that this exception is not extended to anything but rain.

There are ten parts of speech, and they are all troublesome. An average sentence, in a German newspaper, is a sublime and impressive curiosity; it occupies a quarter of a column; it contains all the ten-parts of speech—not in regular order, but mixed; it is built mainly of compound words constructed by the writer on the spot, and not to be found in any dictionary—six or seven words compacted into one, without joint or seam—that is, without hyphens; it treats of fourteen or fifteen different subjects, each enclosed in a parenthesis of its own, with here and there extra parentheses which re-enclose three or four of the minor parentheses, making pens within pens; finally, all the parentheses and re-parentheses are massed together between a couple of king-parentheses, one of which is placed in the first line of the majestic sentence and the other in the middle of the last line of it—after which comes the verb, and you find out for the first time what the man has been talking about; and after the verb—merely by way of ornament, as far as I can make out,—the writer shovels in "haben sind gewesen gehabt haben geworden sein," or words to that effect, and the monument is finished. I suppose that this closing hurrah is in the nature of the flourish to a man's signature—not necessary, but pretty. German books are easy enough to read when you hold them before the looking-glass or stand on your head,—so as to reverse the construction,—but I think that to learn to read and understand a German newspaper is a thing which must always remain an impossibility to a foreigner.

Yet even the German books are not entirely free from attacks of the Parenthesis distemper—though they are usually so mild as to cover only a few lines, and therefore when you at last get down to the verb it carries some meaning to your mind because you are able to remember a good deal of what has gone before.

Now here is a sentence from a popular and excellent German novel,—with a slight parenthesis in it. I will make a perfectly literal translation, and throw in the parenthesis-marks and some hyphens for the assistance of the reader,—though in the original there are no parenthesis-marks or hyphens, and the reader is left to flounder through to the remote verb the best way he can:

"But when he, upon the street, the (in-satin-and-silk-covered-   now-very-unconstrainedly-after-the-newest-fashion-dressed) government counsellor's wife met," etc., etc.[1]

That is from "The Old Mamselle's Secret," by Mrs. Marlitt. And that sentence is constructed upon the most approved German model. You observe how far that verb is from the reader's base of operations; well, in a German newspaper they put their verb away over on the next page; and I have heard that sometimes after stringing along on exciting preliminaries and parentheses for a column or two, they get in a hurry and have to go to press without getting to the verb at all. Of course, then, the reader is left in a very exhausted and ignorant state.

We have the Parenthesis disease in our literature, too; and one may see cases of it every day in our books and newspapers: but with us it is the mark and sign of an unpractised writer or a cloudy intellect, whereas with the Germans it is doubtless the mark and sign of a practised pen and of the presence of that sort of luminous intellectual fog which stands for clearness among these people. For surely it is not clearness,—it necessarily can't be clearness. Even a jury would have penetration enough to discover that. A writer's ideas must be a good deal confused, a good deal out of line and sequence, when he starts out to say that a man met a counsellor's wife in the street, and then right in the midst of this so simple undertaking halts these approaching people and makes them stand still until he jots down an inventory of the woman's dress. That is manifestly absurd. It reminds a person of those dentists who secure your instant and breathless interest in a tooth by taking a grip on it with the forceps, and then stand there and drawl through a tedious anecdote before they give the dreaded jerk. Parentheses in literature and dentistry are in bad taste.

The Germans have another kind of parenthesis, which they make by splitting a verb in two and putting half of it at the beginning of an exciting chapter and the other half at the end of it. Can any one conceive of anything more confusing than that? These things are called "separable verbs." The German grammar is blistered all over with separable verbs; and the wider the two portions of one of them are spread apart, the better the author of the crime is pleased with his performance. A favorite one is reiste ab,—which means, departed. Here is an example which I culled from a novel and reduced to English:

"The trunks being now ready, he DE- after kissing his mother and sisters, and once more pressing to his bosom his adored Gretchen, who, dressed in simple white muslin, with a single tuberose in the ample folds of her rich brown hair, had tottered feebly down the

13

stairs, still pale from the terror and excitement of the past evening, but longing to lay her poor aching head yet once again upon the breast of him whom she loved more dearly than life itself, PARTED."

However, it is not well to dwell too much on the separable verbs. One is sure to lose his temper early; and if he sticks to the subject, and will not be warned, it will at last either soften his brain or petrify it. Personal pronouns and adjectives are a fruitful nuisance in this language, and should have been left out. For instance, the same sound, sie, means you, and it means she, and it means her, and it means it, and it means they, and it means them. Think of the ragged poverty of a language which has to make one word do the work of six,—and a poor little weak thing of only three letters at that. But mainly, think of the exasperation of never knowing which of these meanings the speaker is trying to convey. This explains why, whenever a person says sie to me, I generally try to kill him, if a stranger.

Now observe the Adjective. Here was a case where simplicity would have been an advantage; therefore, for no other reason, the inventor of this language complicated it all he could. When we wish to speak of our "good friend or friends," in our enlightened tongue, we stick to the one form and have no trouble or hard feeling about it; but with the German tongue it is different. When a German gets his hands on an adjective, he declines it, and keeps on declining it until the common sense is all declined out of it. It is as bad

14

as Latin. He says, for instance:

SINGULAR.

Nominative—Mein guter Freund, my good friend.
Genitive—Meines guten Freundes, of my good friend.
Dative—Meinem guten Freund, to my good friend.
Accusative—Meinen guten Freund, my good friend.
PLURAL.

N.—Meine guten Freunde, my good friends.
G.—Meiner guten Freunde, of my good friends.
D.—Meinen guten Freunden, to my good friends.
A.—Meine guten Freunde, my good friends.

Now let the candidate for the asylum try to memorize those variations, and see how soon he will be elected. One might better go without friends in Germany than take all this trouble about them. I have shown what a bother it is to decline a good (male) friend; well, this is only a third of the work, for there is a variety of new distortions of the adjective to be learned when the object is feminine, and still another when the object is neuter. Now there are more adjectives in this language than there are black cats in Switzerland, and they must all be as elaborately declined as the examples above suggested. Difficult?— troublesome?—these words cannot describe it. I heard a Californian student in Heidelberg, say, in one of his calmest moods, that he would rather decline two drinks than one German adjective.

The inventor of the language seems to have taken pleasure in complicating it in every way he could think of. For instance, if one is casually referring to a house, Haus, or a horse, Pferd, or a dog, Hund, he spells these words as I have indicated; but if he is referring to them in the Dative case, he sticks on a foolish and unnecessary e and spells them Hause, Pferde, Hunde. So, as an added e often signifies the plural, as the s does with us, the new student is likely to go on for a month making twins out of a Dative dog before he discovers his mistake; and on the other hand, many a new student who could ill afford loss, has bought and paid for two dogs and only got one of them, because he ignorantly bought that dog in the Dative singular when he really supposed he was talking plural,—which left the law on the seller's side, of course, by the strict rules of grammar, and therefore a suit for recovery could not lie.

In German, all the Nouns begin with a capital letter. Now that is a good idea; and a good idea, in this language, is necessarily conspicuous from its lonesomeness. I consider this capitalizing of nouns a good idea, because by reason of it you are almost always able to tell a noun the minute you see it. You fall into error occasionally, because you mistake the name of a person for the name of a thing, and waste a good deal of time trying to dig a meaning out of it. German names almost always do mean something, and this helps to deceive the student. I translated a passage one day, which said that "the infuriated tigress broke loose and utterly ate up the unfortunate fir-forest,"

(Tannenwald.) When I was girding up my loins to doubt this, I found out that Tannenwald, in this instance, was a man's name.

Every noun has a gender, and there is no sense or system in the distribution; so the gender of each must be learned separately and by heart. There is no other way. To do this, one has to have a memory like a memorandum book. In German, a young lady has no sex, while a turnip has. Think what overwrought reverence that shows for the turnip, and what callous disrespect for the girl. See how it looks in print—I translate this from a conversation in one of the best of the German Sunday-school books:

"Gretchen. Wilhelm, where is the turnip?

"Wilhelm. She has gone to the kitchen.

"Gretchen. Where is the accomplished and beautiful English maiden?

"Wilhelm. It has gone to the opera."

To continue with the German genders: a tree is male, its buds are female, its leaves are neuter; horses are sexless, dogs are male, cats are female,—Tom-cats included, of course; a person's mouth, neck, bosom, elbows, fingers, nails, feet, and body, are of the male sex, and his head is male or neuter according to the word selected to signify it, and not according to the sex of the individual who wears it,—for in Germany all the women wear either male heads or sexless ones; a person's nose, lips, shoulders, breast, hands, hips, and toes are of the female sex; and his hair, ears, eyes, chin, legs, knees, heart, and conscience, haven't any sex at

17

all. The inventor of the language probably got what he knew about a conscience from hearsay.

Now, by the above dissection, the reader will see that in Germany a man may think he is a man, but when he comes to look into the matter closely, he is bound to have his doubts; he finds that in sober truth he is a most ridiculous mixture; and if he ends by trying to comfort himself with the thought that he can at least depend on a third of this mess as being manly and masculine, the humiliating second thought will quickly remind him that in this respect he is no better off than any woman or cow in the land.

In the German it is true that by some oversight of the inventor of the language, a Woman is a female; but a Wife, (Weib,) is not,—which is unfortunate. A Wife, here, has no sex; she is neuter; so, according to the grammar, a fish is he, his scales are she, but a fishwife is neither. To describe a wife as sexless, may be called under-description; that is bad enough, but over-description is surely worse. A German speaks of an Englishman as the Engländer; to change the sex, he adds inn, and that stands for Englishwoman,— Engländerinn. That seems descriptive enough, but still it is not exact enough for a German; so he precedes the word with that article which indicates that the creature to follow is feminine, and writes it down thus: "die Englanderinn,"—which means "the she-Englishwoman." I consider that that person is over-described.

Well, after the student has learned the sex of a great number of nouns, he is still in a difficulty, because he finds it impossible to persuade his tongue to refer to things as "he" and "she," and "him" and "her," which it has been always accustomed to refer to as "it." When he even frames a German sentence in his mind, with the hims and hers in the right places, and then works up his courage to the utterance-point, it is no use,— the moment he begins to speak his tongue flies the track and all those labored males and females come out as "its." And even when he is reading German to himself, he always calls those things "it;" whereas he ought to read in this way:

Tale of the Fishwife and Its Sad Fate.[2]

It is a bleak Day. Hear the Rain, how he pours, and the Hail, how he rattles; and see the Snow, how he drifts along, and oh the Mud, how deep he is! Ah the poor Fishwife, it is stuck fast in the Mire; it has dropped its Basket of Fishes; and its Hands have been cut by the Scales as it seized some of the falling Creatures; and one Scale has even got into its Eye, and it cannot get her out. It opens its Mouth to cry for Help; but if any Sound comes out of him, alas he is drowned by the raging of the Storm. And now a Tomcat has got one of the Fishes and she will surely escape with him. No, she bites off a Fin, she holds her in her Mouth,—will she swallow her? No, the Fishwife's brave Mother-Dog deserts his Puppies and rescues the Fin,—which he eats, himself, as his Reward. O, horror, the Lightning has struck the

19

Fishbasket; he sets him on Fire; see the Flame, how she licks the doomed Utensil with her red and angry Tongue; now she attacks the helpless Fishwife's Foot,—she burns him up, all but the big Toe and even she is partly consumed; and still she spreads, still she waves her fiery Tongues; she attacks the Fishwife's Leg and destroys it; she attacks its Hand and destroys her; she attacks its poor worn Garment and destroys her also; she attacks its Body and consumes him; she wreathes herself about its Heart and it is consumed; next about its Breast, and in a Moment she is a Cinder; now she reaches its Neck,—he goes; now its Chin,—it goes; now its Nose,—she goes. In another Moment, except Help come, the Fishwife will be no more. Time presses,—is there none to succor and save? Yes! Joy, joy, with flying Feet the she-Englishwoman comes! But alas, the generous she-Female is too late: where now is the fated Fishwife? It has ceased from its Sufferings, it has gone to a better Land; all that is left of it for its loved Ones to lament over, is this poor smouldering Ash-heap. Ah, woful, woful Ash-heap! Let us take him up tenderly, reverently, upon the lowly Shovel, and bear him to his long Rest, with the Prayer that when he rises again it will be in a Realm where he will have one good square responsible Sex, and have it all to himself, instead of having a mangy lot of assorted Sexes scattered all over him in Spots.

There, now, the reader can see for himself that this pronoun-business is a very awkward thing for the unaccustomed tongue.

20

I suppose that in all languages the similarities of look and sound between words which have no similarity in meaning are a fruitful source of perplexity to the foreigner. It is so in our tongue, and it is notably the case in the German. Now there is that troublesome word vermählt: to me it has so close a resemblance,—either real or fancied,—to three or four other words, that I never know whether it means despised, painted, suspected, or married; until I look in the dictionary, and then I find it means the latter. There are lots of such words, and they are a great torment. To increase the difficulty there are words which seem to resemble each other, and yet do not; but they make just as much trouble as if they did. For instance,-there is the word vermiethen, (to let, to lease, to hire); and the word verheirathen, (another way of saying to marry.) I heard of an Englishman who knocked at a man's door in Heidelberg and proposed, in the best German he could command, to "verheirathen" that house. Then there are some words which mean one thing when you emphasize the first syllable, but mean something very different if you throw the emphasis on the last syllable. For instance, there is a word which means a runaway, or the act of glancing through a book, according to the placing of the emphasis; and another word which signifies to associate with a man, or to avoid him, according to where you put the emphasis,—and you can generally depend on putting it in the wrong place and getting into trouble.

There are some exceedingly useful words in this language. Schlag, for example; and Zug. There are three-quarters of a column of Schlags in the dictionary, and a column and a half of Zugs. The word Schlag means Blow, Stroke, Dash, Hit, Shock, Clip, Slap, Time, Bar, Coin, Stamp, Kind, Sort, Manner, Way, Apoplexy, Wood-Cutting, Enclosure, Field, Forest-Clearing. This is its simple and exact meaning,—that is to say, its restricted, its fettered meaning; but there are ways by which you can set it free, so that it can soar away, as on the wings of the morning, and never be at rest. You can hang any word you please to its tail, and make it mean anything you want to. You can begin with Schlag-ader, which means artery, and you can hang on the whole dictionary, word by word, clear through the alphabet to Schlag-wasser, which means bilge-water,—and including Schlag-mutter, which means mother-in-law.

Just the same with Zug. Strictly speaking, Zug means Pull, Tug, Draught, Procession, March, Progress, Flight, Direction, Expedition, Train, Caravan, Passage, Stroke, Touch, Line, Flourish, Trait of Character, Feature, Lineament, Chess-move, Organ-stop, Team, Whiff, Bias, Drawer, Propensity, Inhalation, Disposition: but that thing which it does not mean,—when all its legitimate pendants have been hung on, has not been discovered yet.

One cannot over-estimate the usefulness of Schlag and Zug. Armed just with these two, and the word Also, what cannot the foreigner on German soil accomplish? The German word Also is the equivalent of the English phrase "You know," and does not mean anything at all,—in talk, though it sometimes does in print. Every time a German opens his mouth an Also falls out; and every time he shuts it he bites one in two that was trying to get out.

Now, the foreigner, equipped with these three noble words, is master of the situation. Let him talk right along, fearlessly; let him pour his indifferent German forth, and when he lacks for a word, let him heave a Schlag into the vacuum; all the chances are, that it fits it like a plug; but if it doesn't, let him promptly heave a Zug after it; the two together can hardly fail to bung the hole; but if, by a miracle, they should fail, let him simply say Also! and this will give him a moment's chance to think of the needful word. In Germany, when you load your conversational gun it is always best to throw in a Schlag or two and a Zug or two; because it doesn't make any difference how much the rest of the charge may scatter, you are bound to bag something with them. Then you blandly say Also, and load up again. Nothing gives such an air of grace and elegance and unconstraint to a German or an English conversation as to scatter it full of "Also's" or "You knows."

In my note-book I find this entry:

July 1.—In the hospital, yesterday, a word of thirteen syllables was successfully removed from a patient,—a North-German from near Hamburg; but as most unfortunately the surgeons had opened him in the wrong place, under the impression that he contained a panorama, he died. The sad event has cast a gloom over the whole community.

That paragraph furnishes a text for a few remarks about one of the most curious and notable features of my subject,—the length of German words. Some German words are so long that they have a perspective. Observe these examples:

Freundschaftsbezeigungen.
Dilletantenaufdringlichkeiten.
Stadtverordnetenversammlungen.

These things are not words, they are alphabetical processions. And they are not rare; one can open a German newspaper any time and see them marching majestically across the page,—and if he has any imagination he can see the banners and hear the music, too. They impart a martial thrill to the meekest subject. I take a great interest in these curiosities. "Whenever I come across a good one, I stuff it and put it in my museum. In this way I have made quite a valuable collection. When I get duplicates, I exchange with other collectors, and thus increase the variety of my stock. Here are some specimens which I lately bought at an auction sale of the effects of a bankrupt bric-a-brac hunter:

Generalstaatsverordnetenversammlungen.
Alterthumswissenschaften.
Kinderbewahrungsanstalten.
Unabhaengigkeitserklaerungen.

Wiederherstellungsbestrebungen.
Waffenstillstandsunterhandlungen.

Of course when one of these grand mountain ranges goes stretching across the printed page, it adorns and ennobles that literary landscape,—but at the same time it is a great distress to the new student, for it blocks up his way; he cannot crawl under it, or climb over it or tunnel through it. So he resorts to the dictionary for help; but there is no help there. The dictionary must draw the line somewhere,—so it leaves this sort of words out. And it is right, because these long things are hardly legitimate words, but are rather combinations of words, and the inventor of them ought to have been killed. They are compound words, with the hyphens left out. The various words used in building them are in the dictionary, but in a very scattered condition; so you can hunt the materials out, one by one, and get at the meaning at last, but it is a tedious and harrassing business. I have tried this process upon some of the above examples. 'Freundschaftsbezeigungen" seems to be "Friendship demonstrations," which is only a foolish and clumsy way of saying "demonstrations of friendship." "Unabhaengigkeitserklaerungen" seems to be "Independencedeclarations," which is no improvement upon "Declarations of Independence," as far as I can see. "Generalstaatsverordnetenversammlungen" seems to be "Generalstatesrepresentativesmeetings," as nearly as I can get at it,—a mere rhythmical, gushy euphuism for "meetings of the legislature," I judge. We used to have a good deal of this sort of crime in our literature,

25

but it has gone out, now. We used to speak of a thing as a "never-to-be-forgotten" circumstance, instead of cramping it into the simple and sufficient word "memorable" and then going calmly about our business as if nothing had happened. In those days we were not content to embalm the thing and bury it decently, we wanted to build a monument over it.

But in our newspapers the compounding-disease lingers a little to the present day, but with the hyphens left out, in the German fashion. This is the shape it takes: instead of saying "Mr. Simmons, clerk of the county and district courts, was in town yesterday," the new form puts it thus: "Clerk of the County and District Court Simmons was in town yesterday." This saves neither time nor ink, and has an awkward sound besides. One often sees a remark like this in our papers: "Mrs. Assistant District Attorney Johnson returned to her city residence yesterday for the season." That is a case of really unjustifiable compounding; because it not only saves no time or trouble, but confers a title on Mrs. Johnson which she has no right to. But these little instances are trifles indeed, contrasted with the ponderous and dismal German system of piling jumbled compounds together. I wish to submit the following local item, from a Mannheim journal, by way of illustration:

"In the daybeforeyesterdayshortlyaftereleveno'clock Night, the inthistownstandingtavern called "The Wagoner" was downburnt. When the fire to the onthedownburninghouseresting Stork's Nest reached, flew the parent Storks away. But when the bytheraging, firesurrounded Nest itself caught Fire, straightway plunged the quickreturning Mother-Stork into the Flames and died, her Wings over her young ones outspread."

Even the cumbersome German construction is not able to take the pathos out of that picture,—indeed it somehow seems to strengthen it. This item is dated away back yonder months ago. I could have used it sooner, but I was waiting to hear from the Father-Stork. I am still waiting.

"Also!" If I have not shown that the German is a difficult language, I have at least intended to do it. I have heard of an American student who was asked how he was getting along with his German, and who answered promptly: "I am not getting along at all. I have worked at it hard for three level months, and all I have got to show for it is one solitary German phrase,—'Zwei glas,'" (two glasses of beer.) He paused a moment, reflectively, then added with feeling, "But I've got that solid!"

And if I have not also shown that German is a harassing and infuriating study, my execution has been at fault, and not my intent. I heard lately of a worn and sorely tried American student who used to fly to a certain German word for relief when he could bear up under his aggravations no longer,—the only word in the whole language whose sound was sweet and precious to his ear and healing to his lacerated spirit. This was the word Damit. It was only the sound that helped him, not the meaning[3]; and so, at last, when he learned that the emphasis was not on the first syllable, his only stay and support was gone, and he faded away and died.

I think that a description of any loud, stirring, tumultuous episode must be tamer in German than in English. Our descriptive words of this character have such a deep, strong, resonant sound, while their German equivalents do seem so thin and mild and energyless. Boom, burst, crash, roar, storm, bellow, blow, thunder, explosion; howl, cry, shout, yell, groan; battle, hell. These are magnificent words; they have a force and magnitude of sound befitting the things which they describe. But their German equivalents would be ever so nice to sing the children to sleep with, or else my awe-inspiring ears were made for display and not for superior usefulness in analyzing sounds. Would any man want to die in a battle which was called by so tame a term as a Schlacht? Or would not a consumptive feel too much bundled up, who was about to go out, in a shirt collar and a seal ring, into a storm which the bird-song word Gewitter was employed to describe? And observe the strongest of the several German equivalents for explosion,— Ausbruch. Our word Toothbrush is more powerful than that. It seems to me that the Germans could do worse than import it into their language to describe particularly tremendous explosions with. The German word for hell,—Hölle, —sounds more like helly than anything else; therefore, how necessarily chipper, frivolous and unimpressive it is. If a man were told in

German to go there, could he really rise to the dignity of feeling insulted?

Having now pointed out, in detail, the several vices of this language, I now come to the brief and pleasant task of pointing out its virtues. The capitalizing of the nouns, I have already mentioned. But far before this virtue stands another,—that of spelling a word according to the sound of it. After one short lesson in the alphabet, the student can tell how any German word is pronounced, without having to ask; whereas in our language if a student should inquire of us "What does B, O, W, spell?" we should be obliged to reply, "Nobody can tell what it spells, when you set it off by itself,—you can only tell by referring to the context and finding out what it signifies,—whether it is a thing to shoot arrows with, or a nod of one's head, or the forward end of a boat."

There are some German words which are singularly and powerfully effective. For instance, those which describe lowly, peaceful and affectionate home life; those which deal with love, in any and all forms, from mere kindly feeling and honest good will toward the passing stranger, clear up to courtship; those which deal with outdoor Nature, in its softest and loveliest aspects,—with meadows, and forests, and birds and flowers, the fragrance and sunshine of summer, and the moonlight of peaceful winter nights; in a word, those which deal with any and all forms of rest, repose, and peace; those also which deal with the creatures and marvels of fairyland; and lastly and chiefly, in those words which express pathos, is the language surpassingly rich and effective. There are German songs which can make a stranger to the language cry. That shows that the sound of the words is correct,—it interprets the meanings with truth and with exactness; and so the ear is informed, and through the ear, the heart.

The Germans do not seem to be afraid to repeat a word when it is the right one. They repeat it several times, if they choose. That is wise. But in English when we have used a word a couple of times in a paragraph, we imagine we are growing tautological, and so we are weak enough to exchange it for some other word which only approximates exactness, to escape what we wrongly fancy is a greater blemish. Repetition may be bad, but surely inexactness is worse.

There are people in the world who will take a great deal of trouble to point out the faults in a religion or a language, and then go blandly about their business without suggesting any remedy. I am not that kind of a person. I have shown that the German language needs reforming. Very well, I am ready to reform it. At least I am ready to make the proper suggestions. Such a course as this might be immodest in another; but I have devoted upwards of nine full weeks, first and last, to a careful and critical study of this tongue, and thus have acquired a confidence in my ability to reform it which no mere superficial culture could have conferred upon me.

In the first place, I would leave out the Dative Case. It confuses the plurals; and besides, nobody ever knows when he is in the Dative Case, except he discover it by accident,—and then he does not know when or where it was that he got into it, or how long he has been in it, or how he is ever going to get out of it again. The Dative Case is but an ornamental folly,—it is better to discard it.

In the next place, I would move the Verb further up to the front. You may load up with ever so good a Verb, but I notice that you never really bring down a subject with it at the present German range,—you only cripple it. So I insist that this important part of speech should be brought forward to a position where it may be easily seen with the naked eye.

Thirdly, I would import some strong words from the English tongue,—to swear with, and also to use in describing all sorts of vigorous things in a vigorous way.[4]

Fourthly, I would reorganize the sexes, and distribute them according to the will of the Creator. This as a tribute of respect, if nothing else.

Fifthly, I would do away with those great long compounded words; or require the speaker to deliver them in sections, with intermissions for refreshments. To wholly do away with them would be best, for ideas are more easily received and digested when they come one at a time than when they come in bulk. Intellectual

31

food is like any other; it is pleasanter and more beneficial to take it with a spoon than with a shovel.

Sixthly, I would require a speaker to stop when he is done, and not hang a string of those useless "haben sind gewesen gehabt haben geworden seins" to the end of his oration. This sort of gew-gaws undignify a speech, instead of adding a grace. They are therefore an offense, and should be discarded.

Seventhly, I would discard the Parenthesis. Also the re-Parenthesis, the re-re-parenthesis, and the re-re-re-re-re-parentheses, and likewise the final wide-reaching all-enclosing King-parenthesis. I would require every individual, be he high or low, to unfold a plain straightforward tale, or else coil it and sit on it and hold his peace. Infractions of this law should be punishable with death.

And eighthly and lastly, I would retain Zug and Schlag, with their pendants, and discard the rest of the vocabulary. This would simplify the language.

I have now named what I regard as the most necessary and important changes. These are perhaps all I could be expected to name for nothing; but there are other suggestions which I can and will make in case my proposed application shall result in my being formally employed by the government in the work of reforming the language.

My philological studies have satisfied me that a

gifted person ought to learn English (barring spelling and pronouncing), in 30 hours, French in 30 days, and German in 30 years. It seems manifest, then, that the latter tongue ought to be trimmed down and repaired. If it is to remain as it is, it ought to be gently and reverently set aside among the dead languages, for only the dead have time to learn it.

A Fourth of July Oration in the German Tongue, delivered at a Banquet of the Anglo-American Club of students by the Author of this book.

Gentlemen: Since I arrived, a month ago, in this old wonderland, this vast garden of Germany, my English tongue has so often proved a useless piece of baggage to me, and so troublesome to carry around, in a country where they haven't the checking system for luggage, that I finally set to work, last week, and learned the German language. Also! Es freŭt mich dass dies so ist, denn es muss, in ein hauptsächlich degree, höflich sein, dass man aŭf ein occasion like this, sein Rede in die Sprache des Landes worin he boards, aŭssprechen soll. Dafür habe ich, aŭs reinische Verlegenheit,—no Vergangenheit,—no, I mean Höflichkeit,—aŭs reinische Höflichkeit habe ich resolved to tackle this business in the German language, ŭm Gottes willen! Also! Sie müssen so freŭndlich sein, ŭnd verzeih mich die interlarding von ein oder zwei Englischer Worte, hie ŭnd da, denn ich finde dass die deŭtche is not a very copious language, and so when you've really got anything to say, you've got to draw on a language that can stand the strain.

Wenn aber man kann nicht meinem Rede verstehen, so werde ich ihm später dasselbe übersetz, wenn er solche Dienst verlangen wollen haben werden sollen sein hätte. (I don't know what wollen haben werden sollen sein hätte means, but I notice they always put it at the end of a German sentence—merely for general literary gorgeousness, I suppose.)

This is a great and justly honored day,—a day which is worthy of the veneration in which it is held by the true patriots of all climes and nationalities,—a day which offers a fruitful theme for thought and speech; ŭnd meinem Freŭnde,—no, meinen Freŭden, — meines Freŭndes,—well, take your choice, they're all the same price; I don't know which one is right,—also! ich habe gehabt haben worden gewesen sein, as Goethe says, in his Paradise Lost, —ich,—ich,—that is to say,—ich,—but let us change cars.

Also! Die Anblick so viele Grossbrittanischer ŭnd Amerikanischer hier zusammengetroffen in Bruderliche concord, ist zwar a welcome and inspiriting spectacle. And what has moved you to it? Can the terse German tongue rise to the expression of this impulse? Is it Freŭnd-schafts-be-zei-gŭn-gen-stadt-ver-ord-ne-ten-ve r-samm-lun-gen-fa-mi-li-en-eigen-thüm-lich-kei-ten? Nein, o nein! This is a crisp and noble word, but it fails to pierce the marrow of the impulse which has gathered this friendly meeting and produced diese Anblick,—eine Anblick welche ist gŭt zu sehen,—gŭt für die Aŭgen in a foreign land and a far country,—

eine Anblick solche als in die gewönliche Heidelberger phrase nennt man ein "schönes Aussicht!" Ja, freilich natürlich wahrscheinlich ebensowohl! Also! Die Aussicht aŭf dem Königstuhl mehr grösserer ist, aber geistlische sprechend nicht so schön, lob' Gott! Because sie sind hier zusammengetroffen, in Bruderlichem concord, ein grossen Tag zu feiern, whose high benefits were not for one land and one locality only, but have conferred a measure of good upon all lands that know liberty to day, and love it. Hŭndert Jahre vorüber, waren die Engländer ŭnd die Amerikaner Feinde; aber heŭte sind sie herzlichen Freŭnde, Gott sei Dank! May this good fellowship endure; may these banners here blended in amity, so remain; may they never any more wave over opposing hosts, or be stained with blood which was kindred, is kindred, and always will be kindred, until a line drawn upon a map shall be able to say, "This bars the ancestral blood from flowing in the veins of the descendant!"

1. Wenn er aber auf der Strasse der in Sammt und Seide gehüllten jetz sehr ungenirt nach der neusten mode gekleideten Regierungsrathin begegnet."

2. I capitalize the nouns, in the German (and ancient English) fashion.

3. It merely means, in its general sense, "herewith."

4. "Verdammt," and its variations and enlargements, are words which have plenty of meaning, but the sounds are so mild and ineffectual that German ladies can use them without sin. German ladies who could not be induced to commit a sin by

any persuasion or compulsion, promptly rip out one of these harmless little words when they tear their dresses or don't like the soup. It sounds about as wicked as our "My gracious." German ladies are constantly saying, "Ach! Gott!" "Mein Gott!" "Gott in Himmel!" "Herr Gott!" "Der Herr Jesus!" etc. They think our ladies have the same custom, perhaps, for I once heard a gentle and lovely old German lady say to a sweet young American girl, "The two languages are so alike—how pleasant that is; we say 'Ach! Gott!' you say 'Goddam.'"

THE END

RISE OF DOUAI

TWITTER : @RISEOFDOUAI

SIGHT BY ELSIE BENEDICT
(PAPERBACK) ISBN-10: 1480081272

- THE ART OF WAR BY MR SUN TZU (PAPERBACK) ISBN-10: 1480082007
- MACBETH BY MR WILLIAM SHAKESPEARE (PAPERBACK) ISBN-10: 1480060682

- A CHRISTMAS CAROL BY MR CHARLES DICKENS ISBN-10: 1481194755
- CREATING CAPITAL: MONEY-MAKING AS AN AIM IN BUSINESS BY MR FREDRICK L LIPMAN ISBN-10: 1481158996
- GETTING GOLD: A PRACTICAL TREATISE FOR PROSPECTORS, MINERS, AND STUDENTS BY MR JOSEPH COLIN FRANCIS JOHNSON ISBN-10: 1481090984
- THE INTERPRETATION OF DREAMS BY MR SIGMUND FREUD ISBN-10: 1481134558

- THE COMMUNIST MANIFESTO BY MR KARL MARX AND MR FRIDRICK ENGLES ISBN-10: 1480112445
- THE PRINCE BY MR NICCOLO MACHIAVELLI ISBN-10: 1480119601
- THE WAY TO WEALTH BY MR BENJAMIN FRANKLIN ISBN-10: 1480099651
- THE ART OF MONEY GETTING - OR GOLDEN RULES FOR MAKING MONEY (SUCCESS PRINCIPLES) BY MR PHINEAS TAYLOR BARNUM ISBN-10: 1480138622

Twitter : **@RiseofDouai**

Made in the USA
Middletown, DE
27 July 2022